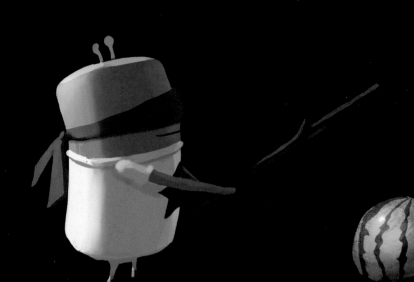
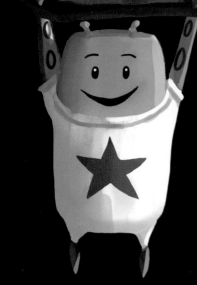

Thanks, Mom and Dad, for always supporting me even if you would
not have let me keep an alien. And to my wife, Rachael: thanks for
being my source of happiness and for being my best friend. —G.F.

STERLING CHILDREN'S BOOKS
New York

An Imprint of Sterling Publishing
1166 Avenue of the Americas
New York, NY 10036

Text © 2015 by Tammi Sauer
Illustrations © 2015 by Goro Fujita
The artwork for this book was created using Adobe Photoshop.
Designed by Andrea Miller

ISBN 978-1-4549-1129-6

Distributed in Canada by Sterling Publishing
c/o Canadian Manda Group, 664 Annette Street
Toronto, Ontario, Canada M6S 2C8
Distributed in the United Kingdom by GMC Distribution Services
Castle Place, 166 High Street, Lewes, East Sussex, England BN7 1XU
Distributed in Australia by Capricorn Link (Australia) Pty. Ltd.
P.O. Box 704, Windsor, NSW 2756, Australia

For information about custom editions, special sales,
and premium and corporate purchases,
please contact Sterling Special Sales at 800-805-5489
or specialsales@sterlingpublishing.com.

Manufactured in China
Lot #:
10 9 8 7 6 5 4 3 2 1
05/15

www.sterlingpublishing.com/kids

YOUR ALIEN

by Tammi Sauer
illustrated by Goro Fujita

STERLING CHILDREN'S BOOKS
New York

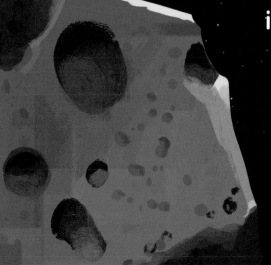

You will be looking out your window
when something wonderful comes your way.

You will want to keep him.

You'll have to break the news to your parents.

Luckily, they won't notice
what they just agreed to.

Your alien will
follow you to school.

He'll love the art supplies
and the water fountain.

But Mr. Binky will make
him a little nervous.

Your classmates will think your alien is awesome.

As for your teacher?
She'll think she needs new glasses.

At the end of the school day, your alien will want to go exploring.

You'll see ordinary things in a brand-new way.

After a while, your alien will realize he's hungry.
The two of you will race home for dinner.

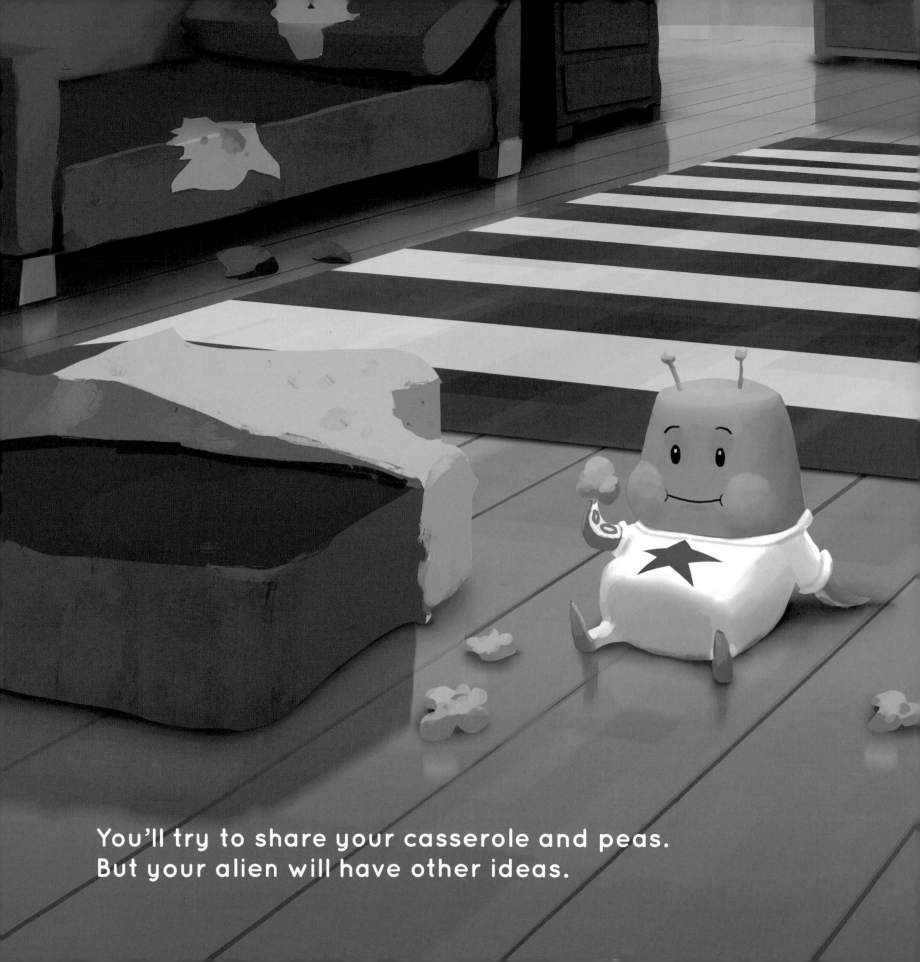

You'll try to share your casserole and peas.
But your alien will have other ideas.

Once you deal with the mess,
you'll notice something is wrong with your alien.

You'll try to make him feel better,
but nothing seems to work.
Not even your robot jammies will do the trick.

You'll both be tired and ready for a bedtime story.

Then your mom and dad will
kiss you good night.

This will make your alien sniffle.
And that will make you sniffle, too.

When you turn off your light, you'll notice
something about your alien right away.

MEEP!

OOG!

You'll quickly turn on the light.
Then you will give your alien a hug.

This will make you think about other hugs.
And, for the first time, you'll know exactly
what your alien needs.

You'll turn on every light in the house.

You'll also decide to add a few extras here and there.

This will attract some attention.

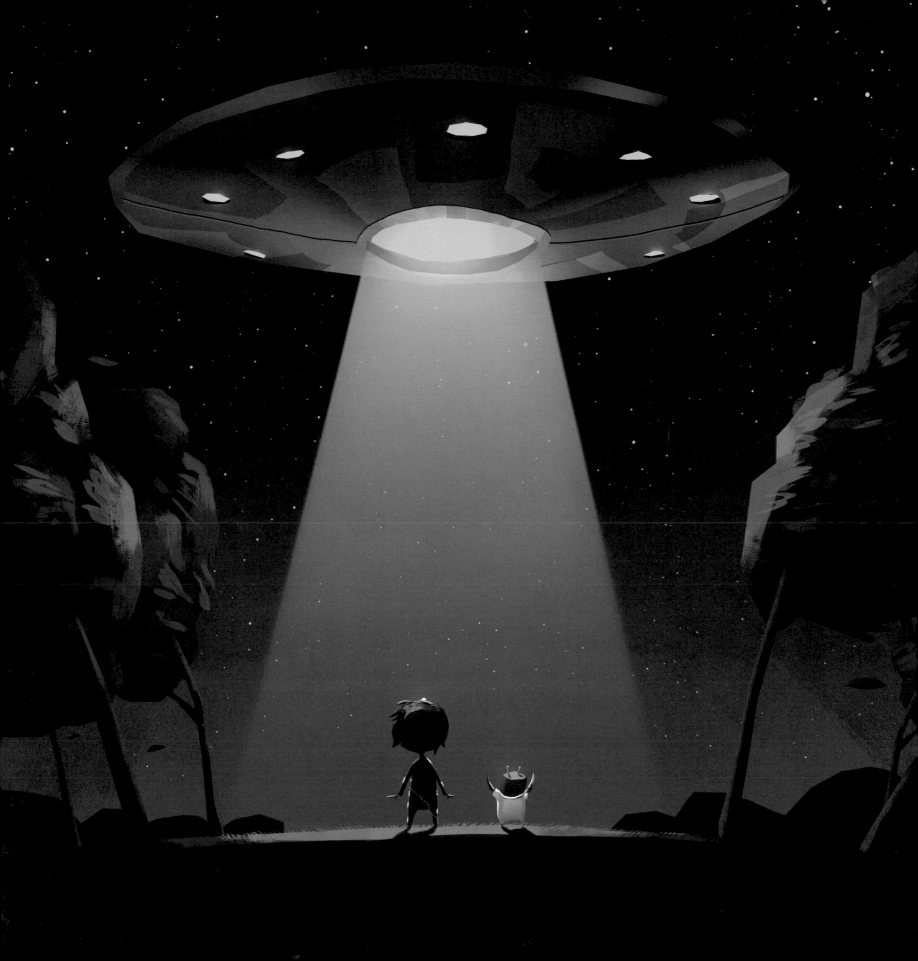

The reunion scene will be out of this world.

Then you and your alien will wave good-bye.

You'll feel like you could really use a hug.

And you will be looking out your window....

BAT

DINO MAMA

FOUR

...when something wonderful comes your way.

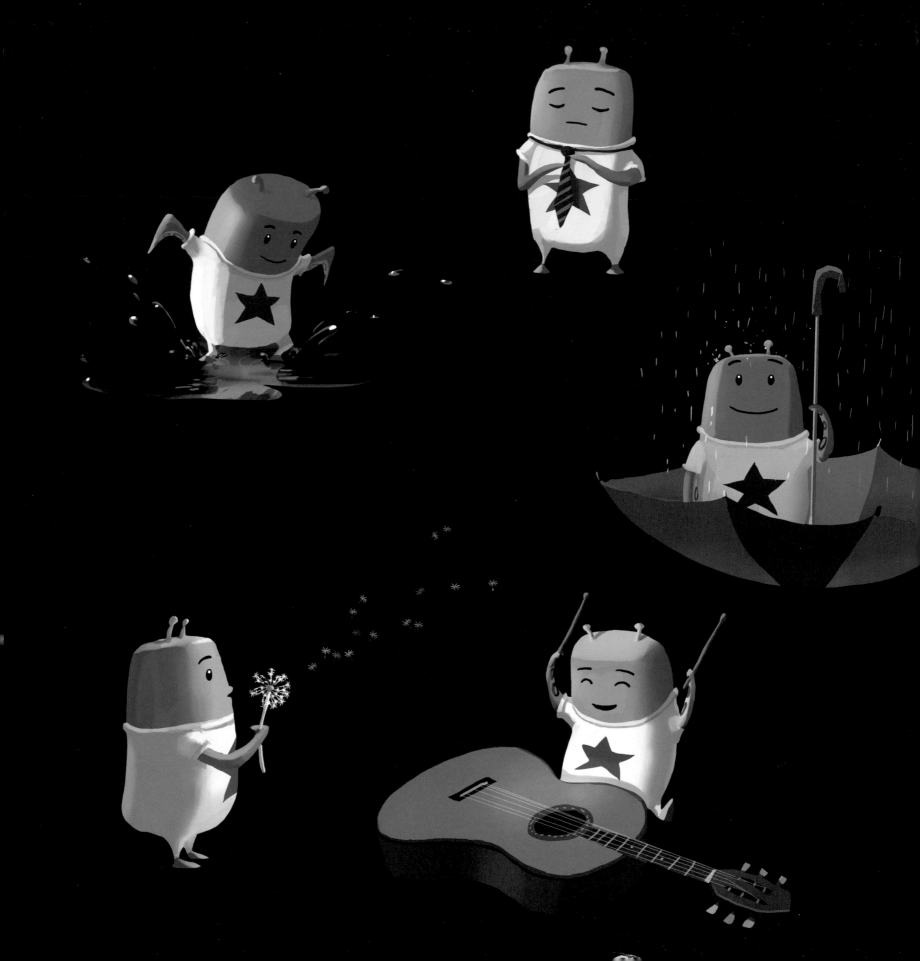